Henrietta smiled sweetly at her fa
got enough money to buy *Hippo*

Dad nodded. 'I know, Mum didn't give you any pocket money this week, did she?'

Henrietta shook her head.

Dad bent down. 'Do you know what I think, Henrietta?'

'What?'

Dad grinned. 'I think you should learn to keep your room tidy, so you would get your pocket money. Then you WOULD be able to buy *Hippo Fun*, EVERY week!'

Henrietta's Pocket Money is the fourth title in a series of books about the mischievous Henrietta and her family.

Also available by Stan Cullimore,
and published by Young Corgi Books:

HENRIETTA AND THE TOOTH FAIRY
HENRIETTA'S BUBBLE TROUBLE
HENRIETTA AND THE GHOST CHASE

Henrietta's POCKET MONEY

Stan Cullimore

Illustrated by John Farman

YOUNG CORGI BOOKS

HENRIETTA'S POCKET MONEY
A YOUNG CORGI BOOK : 0 552 52828 5

First published in Great Britain by Piccadilly Press Ltd

PRINTING HISTORY
Young Corgi edition published 1995

Young Corgi Books are published by Transworld Publishers Ltd,
61–63 Uxbridge Road, Ealing, London W5 5SA,
in Australia by Transworld Publishers (Australia) Pty Ltd,
15–25 Helles Avenue, Moorebank, NSW 2170,
and in New Zealand by Transworld Publishers (NZ) Ltd,
3 William Pickering Drive, Albany, Auckland.

Printed and bound in Great Britain by
Cox & Wyman Ltd, Reading, Berkshire

CONTENTS

STORY ONE:
POCKET MONEY 1

STORY TWO:
THE GREAT DETECTIVE 14

STORY THREE:
THE QUIET COMPETITION 27

STORY FOUR:
DANIEL'S BOAT 40

STORY ONE

POCKET MONEY

'How much money have you got, Henrietta?' asked Daniel.

Henrietta ignored him. She was busy reading *Hippo Fun*.

Daniel put down the cloth he was holding and sighed. 'Because when Mum pays me for doing the dusting – I'll have saved FIVE pounds!'

Henrietta ignored him again.

Suddenly she burst out laughing. 'I LOVE *Hippo Fun*. I can't wait to read this week's copy!' She groaned. 'Ratburgers! I've just remembered – I won't BE able to read this week's copy. I haven't got any money.'

Daniel smiled his most sensible smile. 'That's because you don't EARN it, like I do.'

'No, it isn't,' muttered Henrietta. 'It's because Mum said I couldn't have any pocket money. It's not my fault if my room is ALWAYS messy!'

She thought for a moment.

'Why don't YOU buy *Hippo Fun* this week, Daniel?'

Daniel frowned. 'What for?'

'For ME!'

Daniel shook his head. 'I can't, I'm saving up.'

Henrietta smiled sweetly. 'Please, Daniel. I'll make you some of my SPECIAL chocolate marshmallow cakes . . .'

'With Smarties on top?'

Henrietta nodded.

Daniel licked his lips. But then shook his head again. 'It's no good, Henrietta, you can't bribe me. I'm saving up. If you want some money, you'll have to earn it – like I do!'

Henrietta was just about to stick out her tongue at her sensible brother, when Dad put his head round the door. 'Do either of you two want to come to the shops with me?'

'YES, PLEASE!' shouted Daniel and Henrietta together. 'Well, you'll need your coats,' said Dad. 'It's very windy outside!'

Henrietta smiled sweetly at her father. 'I haven't got enough money to buy *Hippo Fun*, Dad.'

Dad nodded. 'I know, Mum didn't give you any pocket money this week, did she?'

Henrietta shook her head.

Dad bent down. 'Do you know what I think, Henrietta.'

'What?'

Dad grinned. 'I think you should learn to keep your room tidy, so you get your pocket money. Then you WOULD be able to buy *Hippo Fun*, EVERY week!'

'Thanks for NOTHING, Dad. At this rate I'll never read *Hippo Fun* again!'

Henrietta started stomping across the room and was about to slam the living room door when she caught her father's eye. 'I'll just get my coat,' she said weakly.

It was in her bedroom somewhere. All she had to do was find it!

* * *

Ten minutes later they were all walking down the road towards the shops.

Henrietta was very quiet. She was trying to work out a way of persuading someone to buy her *Hippo Fun*.

It wouldn't be easy. Dad had already told her that he wasn't going to, until her room was tidy. But by that time there would be no more *Hippo Fun* left in the shop!

She looked at Daniel.

He was staring at the piece of paper he was holding in his hand.

It was a five pound note.

Daniel had never had one of them before. His father had changed it for the pile of coins he had saved in his piggy bank.

'Daniel,' said Dad, 'don't hold money in your hand. You might drop it – people do, all the time! Why don't you let me take care of it.'

'I'll be careful, Dad. I'm not like Henrietta. I'll put it in my pocket.'

'I never lose MY money,' said Henrietta.

Daniel grinned. 'That's because you never have any!'

'No, it isn't,' replied Henrietta. 'It's because I always spend it as soon as I get it!'

Dad laughed. 'So does your mother!'

He stopped outside a fruit shop. 'You two wait a minute, while I go in here.' He disappeared into the shop.

'The only way YOU would ever get any money,' said Daniel, 'is by finding it. You're too lazy to earn any – not like ME!'

Henrietta stared at the pavement thoughtfully. Daniel had just given her an idea. If she found any money that had been dropped, she might get a reward.

She looked all around to see if anybody HAD dropped some.

But sadly they hadn't. It seemed the only thing that people dropped in the High Street was litter.

'Here we are!' said Dad coming out of the shop with a large bag full of green bananas. 'Would anybody like one of these?'

'Yes, please!' shouted Henrietta,

dancing around the pavement.

Daniel didn't reply. He was too busy thinking about all the five pound notes he would have, if he saved up for the rest of his life.

Suddenly Henrietta stopped dancing around and sighed. They were walking past the papershop. And in the window was this week's copy of *Hippo Fun*.

Dad gave her a banana. 'Eat this. It'll cheer you up,' he said.

He also gave one to Daniel.

'WOWW!' exclaimed Henrietta.

Dad smiled. 'I thought that a green banana would cheer you up, Henrietta.'

Henrietta shook her head. 'It's not that – LOOK!' She pointed.

Daniel looked, and then . . . looked again.

'What's it doing up there?' he squawked.

His five pound note was flying through the air, on its way up to the sky.

'It dropped out of your pocket when you took your hand out to get the banana,' said Henrietta. 'And the wind did the rest.' She shook her head. 'You were right, Dad, if you drop your money – you DO lose it.'

Daniel stared at the five pound note as it rose higher and higher.

He opened his mouth, but no sound came out.

Henrietta finished her banana, and

BANK of ENGLAND
FIVE POUNDS

thought about having another.

Suddenly she blinked. There was something tickling the top of her nose. It was a tiny piece of green banana.

She tried to wipe it away with the banana skin. But it was too late.

'Aaah . . . aaah . . . ATISHOO!' She did a Henrietta hypersneeze that blew the green banana skin high into the sky.

* * *

'YOU'RE A GENIUS, Henrietta!' shouted Daniel.

Henrietta opened her eyes. 'Why?'

At that moment something landed on her head. 'Ooof!' she muttered.

Daniel bent down and picked it up. It was a rolled up green banana skin.

He unrolled it.

There, inside it, was a five pound note!

He shook his head. 'That was amazing, the way you sneezed that banana skin up into the air so that it would hit my five pound note. You're incredible, Henrietta!'

Henrietta looked puzzled. 'Am I?'

Dad laughed. 'I think Henrietta deserves a reward, don't you, Daniel?'

Daniel gulped. 'Does she?'

'Yes,' replied Dad. 'And I know what she would like . . .'

'*Hippo Fun*', shouted Henrietta. 'Yippee!'

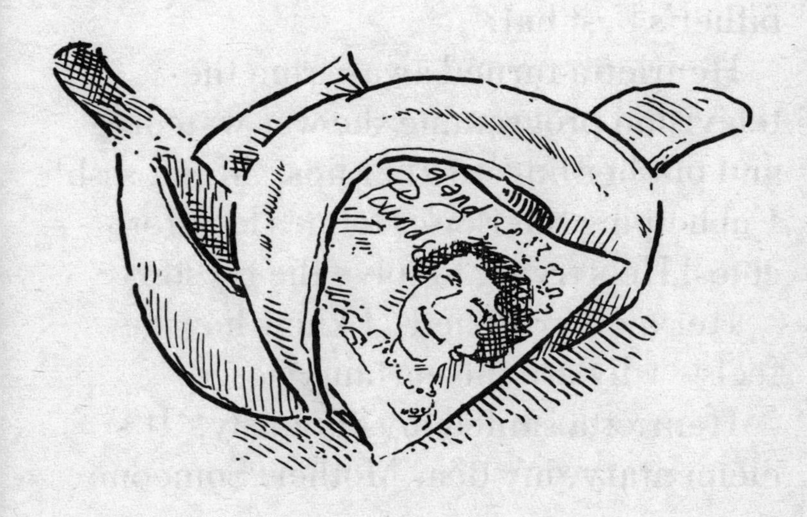

STORY TWO

THE GREAT DETECTIVE

'Henrietta. Why are you wearing your father's best hat?'

Henrietta turned away from the television programme she was watching and put her finger to her lips. 'Mum, sssh! I'm helping Sherlock Holmes look for clues! He's trying to solve the mystery.'

Her mother sighed. 'I know how he feels – why are the curtains closed?'

Henrietta smiled mysteriously. 'It's elementary, my dear Mother. Someone closed them!'

Her mother nodded. 'I can see that. But the question is, who closed them?'

Henrietta picked up a magnifying glass, which was lying on the sofa next to her. 'I'll look for clues. Like Sherlock Holmes does.' She peered at the curtains.

'Aha,' she cried. 'I now know WHO closed the curtains and WHY!'

'How?' asked her mother, frowning.

'Easy,' giggled Henrietta. 'Because it was me! The sun was too bright. I couldn't see the television properly.'

Her mother laughed. 'For a minute there, I thought you had found some REAL clues!'

Before Henrietta could reply, her mother had pulled open the curtains and let the sunlight come flooding into the room.

Henrietta groaned. 'Mum! Now I can't see what's going to happen next.'

Her mother smiled. 'Now it's MY turn to solve the mystery. I KNOW what's going to happen next. You're going to switch off the television and go outside to play while I hoover the carpet – unless YOU want to do it, of course.'

Henrietta stood up and smiled sweetly. 'No thanks, Mum. I'll go and play in the garden.'

She switched off the television and walked out of the room, still wearing her father's deerstalker, and holding the magnifying glass. She was going to look for clues!

* * *

When she got outside, Henrietta found her sensible brother Daniel playing in the sandpit. He was building a sandcastle. Henrietta watched him for a minute and then began to stare closely at the castle through the magnifying glass.

'Could you please do something for me, Henrietta?' asked Daniel politely.

'What?'

'GET LOST!' yelled Daniel in his loudest voice. Then he looked at the magnifying glass in Henrietta's hand. 'What are you doing with that?'

Henrietta tapped her nose with her finger and looked mysterious. 'I'm looking for clues. I'm trying to solve a mystery.'

Daniel snorted. 'Who do you think you are, Sherlock Holmes? Anyway, what is this mystery?'

'I don't know yet,' replied Henrietta. 'That's what makes it SO mysterious!' She walked down the garden path still staring through the magnifying glass.

Five minutes later, Mum came out of the back door. 'Do either of you two know where Baby-Rose is? I can't find her.'

Henrietta looked pleased. 'At last, a mystery. Don't worry, Mum, I'll find Baby-Rose for you. Now to look for clues!' She began to check the lawn for footprints carefully.

'Baby-Rose WAS helping me build my sandcastle,' said Daniel. He looked slowly round the garden. Then he pointed. 'There she is, by the shed.'

'Well spotted! Thank you, Daniel.' His

mother patted him on the head. 'Maybe you should teach Henrietta a thing or two about detective work!' She went back into the house.

Daniel grinned at Henrietta. 'Some detective YOU are. You couldn't even find an elephant in a matchbox!' Laughing happily at his own joke he went back to building his sandcastle.

Henrietta stuck out her tongue at her sensible brother. 'That WASN'T a real mystery – so it DOESN'T count!' She pulled her father's hat down over her eyes. And went to look for clues in the shed.

*   *   *

Ten minutes later, Mum came out of the back door again. She looked worried.

'Mum,' said Daniel. 'Do you like my sandcastle?'

Mum didn't seem to hear him.

'Because Henrietta says it looks more like a mud pie than a sandcastle!' Henrietta had been patrolling the garden for clues, but mostly she was making snide comments at Daniel.

Henrietta giggled. 'Well, it does! Can I have a biscuit, Mum? I'm hungry.'

Mum sighed. 'I'm sorry, I can't think about sandcastles, or biscuits just now. I can't find my gold ring.'

Henrietta's eyes widened with

surprise. Then, without saying a word, she began to search the ground with the magnifying glass.

Daniel gasped. 'The one that Dad gave

you. The one that was REALLY expensive?'

Mum nodded.

Daniel stood up and wiped the sand from his hands. 'Don't worry, Mum. I'll help you find it. Where were you when you lost it?'

Mum shook her head. 'I didn't LOSE it. I took it off, put it on the table – and now it's gone. I think Baby-Rose must have got hold of it.

Daniel climbed out of the sandpit and

began walking up and down the garden, with his hands behind his back. 'Now how would a PROPER detective find it, it's a VERY small ring. So it won't be easy to see where Baby-Rose has put it.' He thought for a moment.

Suddenly he stopped. Henrietta was bent over his sandcastle staring at it through the magnifying glass. Her nose was only centimetres away from the sand.

'Henrietta, get away from my sandcastle.'

Henrietta stood up and smiled. 'Now this is what I call a REAL mystery. I shall call it: The Mystery of The Sandcastle. Because that is where I saw the first clue.'

'What is it?' asked Daniel. 'Sand!' He laughed at his own joke.

Suddenly he squealed. 'Henrietta, GET OFF!'

Henrietta was poking her finger through the wall of his sandcastle.

'MUM,' he cried. 'Can you tell Henrietta to leave my sandcastle alone while I find your ring.'

At that moment Henrietta grabbed some of the sand from Daniel's castle and held it up in her hand. 'LOOK,' she cried. 'I DID see something.'

Daniel squawked. 'So did I! I saw YOU trying to ruin MY sandcastle!' He folded his arms and glared at Henrietta.

Henrietta looked at him through the magnifying glass for a moment. 'My dear Daniel. Please calm down. I have just solved *The Mystery*. I now KNOW where the ring is!'

Daniel snorted. 'YOU! You're a USELESS detective – you'll never be able to find it!'

Henrietta opened her hand and let the sand fall through her fingers. 'I already

have!' And there, shining in the light, was Mum's gold ring. 'It was in the sandcastle,' she said.

'But . . . how did YOU know where it was?' gasped Daniel.

Henrietta smiled. 'Elementary, my dear Daniel. Baby-Rose took the ring AND she helped you build the sandcastle. We all know how she loves to bury things in the sandpit. For a great detective like ME, the rest was easy!'

Mum laughed. 'Well, thank you very much, Henrietta the Great Detective. Would you like to go into the kitchen and find something else for me?'

Henrietta nodded. 'What?'

'The biscuit tin,' replied Mum. 'I expect after all that hard work we all could do with a nice chocolate biscuit!'

STORY THREE

THE QUIET COMPETITION

'Well done, Daniel,' said his father, standing in the hallway. 'At this rate we'll soon be off to the seaside.'

Daniel put down the suitcase he was holding and scratched his nose. 'Dad, why isn't Henrietta helping us pack the car?'

His father smiled. 'She is, in fact, she's JUST gone to get the suitcase from your room.'

Daniel frowned. 'The big, blue suitcase that was on my bed?'

His father nodded.

'You mean THIS one!' Daniel pointed to the suitcase on the floor.

'YES, I do!' His father scratched his head. 'I wonder what happened to Henrietta?'

Daniel snorted. 'I know what! She'll be hiding until all the hard work has been done.'

'Now Daniel, that's not a very nice thing to say about your sister, is it? Why should Henrietta want to hide?'

Daniel took a deep breath. 'Because she's a sneaky, lazy, good-for-nothing, cheeky little . . .'

But before he could finish what he was saying, the door to the cupboard under the stairs flew open.

'I HEARD that, Daniel,' shouted Henrietta. 'And I am NOT lazy OR sneaky!' She folded her arms and gave her sensible brother a hard stare.

Her father cleared his throat. 'Henrietta. What were you doing in the cupboard under the stairs? I asked you to go and help Daniel.'

Henrietta turned and looked at her father. She gulped. And then blinked. 'Er . . . I was looking for my bucket and spade.'

'You weren't hiding in the cupboard and reading your comic, were you?' asked her father.

Henrietta's eyes widened. 'ME! Hiding! Whatever gave you THAT idea?'

Her father pointed at *Hippo Fun* that Henrietta had just dropped on the floor. 'That!' he said firmly.

'Ratburgers!' muttered Henrietta.

Dad turned to Daniel. 'Come on, we'll go and start packing the car – Henrietta can bring down the rest of the things. On her own!' He turned to Henrietta. 'And DON'T start reading *Hippo Fun* again, young lady.'

Henrietta shook her head. 'I won't, Dad. I promise.' She smiled sweetly. 'I've read it all now, anyway.' With that she ran up the stairs, singing to herself happily.

She LOVED going to the seaside.

* * *

Outside, Mum was standing by the car.

She smiled at Dad. 'Good news. Baby-Rose has just fallen asleep.'

Dad grinned. 'That IS good news! She HATES travelling in the car. It always makes her cry.'

Daniel snorted. 'She won't be asleep for long. The minute Henrietta gets in beside her, she'll wake up. Henrietta can never keep her big mouth shut in the car. Especially when she's excited!'

His mother and father looked at one another. Daniel was right.

Mum smiled. 'I know. We'll have a quiet competition. Whoever is the quietest out of Henrietta and Daniel wins a box of chocolates.'

Daniel grinned. 'Suits me. I'm bound to win. Henrietta's MOUTH is much bigger than her BRAIN! She COULDN'T keep it shut even if she wanted to.'

At that moment the front door opened

and Henrietta walked out carrying three buckets, three spades and a large red beachball.

'Look what I found,' she cried. 'It wouldn't have been much fun at the seaside if we didn't have these!'

'Sssh!' hissed Mum. 'Baby-Rose has just fallen asleep.'

'And we're having a quiet competition,' whispered Daniel.

Henrietta looked puzzled. 'A WHAT?'

'A quiet competition,' said Mum. 'We don't want you or Daniel to wake Baby-Rose up. So whoever is the quietest on the journey, will win a box of chocolates.'

'Which means I will.' Daniel smiled his most sensible smile. 'I'm going to sit and play with my pocket computer – and I won't make a sound.'

'Well, I shall listen to my personal stereo – and I won't make a sound either! So there.' Henrietta quietly stuck out her

tongue at her sensible brother and climbed into the car.

*   *   *

Ten minutes later the car was packed and they were driving towards the motorway. The buckets and spades were lying along the back shelf and Henrietta was holding the red beachball.

The only sound to be heard from the

back seat, was the sound of Baby-Rose snoring.

Suddenly a soft humming noise started up.

'Whatever is that?' asked Dad.

'It's Henrietta. She's humming along to the music on her stereo,' hissed Daniel. 'So I've won the competition!'

Dad shook his head. 'Not yet, Daniel. She hasn't woken Baby-Rose up.'

Mum leant round and tapped Henrietta gently on the knee. Henrietta opened her eyes and jumped, dropping the beachball.

Her mother put her finger to her lips. 'Shhh!'

Henrietta nodded. 'Sorry,' she whispered. She picked up the beachball and closed her eyes again.

The humming noise stopped.

Five minutes later Dad turned to Mum. 'I can hear a sort of thumping

sound, can you?'

Mum nodded. 'I wonder if it's the buckets rolling around in the back?' She turned to Daniel. 'Could you stack all the buckets together please, Daniel.'

Daniel carefully stacked the buckets and sat them back on the shelf behind his seat.

After a minute, Mum frowned. 'I can STILL hear that noise!'

'So can I!' Dad looked puzzled. 'I can't think WHAT it is!'

Daniel suddenly started to giggle. 'I can! It's Henrietta. She's pretending to play the drums on the beachball. I MUST have won the competition this time.'

Suddenly Henrietta opened her eyes and realised what she was doing. The thumping stopped. 'Sorry, Mum!' she whispered. 'I won't do it again.'

She put the beachball on the shelf – and accidentally knocked over the pile of buckets.

Silently, they began to roll towards Daniel's seat.

If they fell off the shelf, they would land on his head.

'Mum,' hissed Daniel. 'HAVE I just won the competition?'

'Not yet, Daniel,' said Mum quietly. 'Baby-Rose is still asleep. We'll give Henrietta ONE more chance. But from now on, if either of you make a SOUND. The other one wins!'

Daniel grinned. 'Good! Henrietta's bound to start making a noise in a minute. Then I get the chocolates. I can't wait!'

He didn't notice the buckets rolling towards him.

But Henrietta did!

She opened her mouth to speak.

'Remember,' said Mum. 'Not a sound

from either of you!'

The buckets had nearly reached the edge of the shelf. In a second they would fall. Right on top of Daniel!

Henrietta waved her arms at her brother, trying to warn him.

He stuck out his tongue, and pulled a face at her.

At that moment, the pile of buckets reached the edge of the shelf.

They fell off. And landed on Daniel's head.

'OooWWWWWWWWWW!' yelled Daniel. 'MY HEAD!'

Baby-Rose opened one eye, looked round the car, and opened her mouth.

'I hope it's a big box of chocolates,' said Henrietta happily over the noise. 'Being quiet makes me hungry!'

STORY FOUR

DANIEL'S BOAT

'Let's GO!' shouted Henrietta as she ran into the kitchen. 'All I have to do is find my boat and I'm ready!' She stopped and looked round the room.

Then she groaned:

Everyone was sitting quietly at the table. And no-one was ready to go out.

'I THOUGHT we were going to the park this morning. To sail our boats!' said Henrietta slowly.

Mum nodded. 'We are, I told you – in a minute.'

'But, you said that HOURS ago.'

Henrietta sat down sadly. Suddenly she frowned. She had just noticed what Daniel was holding. She leant over his shoulder and snatched it out of his hands.

'No wonder I couldn't find MY blue sailing boat,' she cried. 'YOU had it!'

Daniel shook his head. 'This is MY boat now, Henrietta.'

Henrietta laughed. 'No, it isn't, silly. YOURS is red! This is MY boat!'

Daniel gave his sister his most

annoying grown-up smile. 'It WAS your boat, Henrietta . . .' he said sweetly. 'Until you dropped MINE out of the bathroom window and smashed it to pieces. REMEMBER?'

Henrietta stopped laughing. 'Oh, yes. I did, didn't I!' She shrugged. 'I only wanted to see if it could fly!'

Dad put down his newspaper. 'Well it couldn't – so you very kindly GAVE your boat to Daniel. Didn't you?'

'Ratburgers,' groaned Henrietta. 'I'd forgotten about that.' She handed Daniel the boat and put her hands in her pockets.

Daniel grinned. 'I can't wait to sail MY new boat. You can watch me if you like, Henrietta. But I don't think it'll fly! Hehehe.'

Henrietta groaned. 'I don't think I want to go to the park anymore. If I haven't got a boat to sail it's going to be so BOR – ing!'

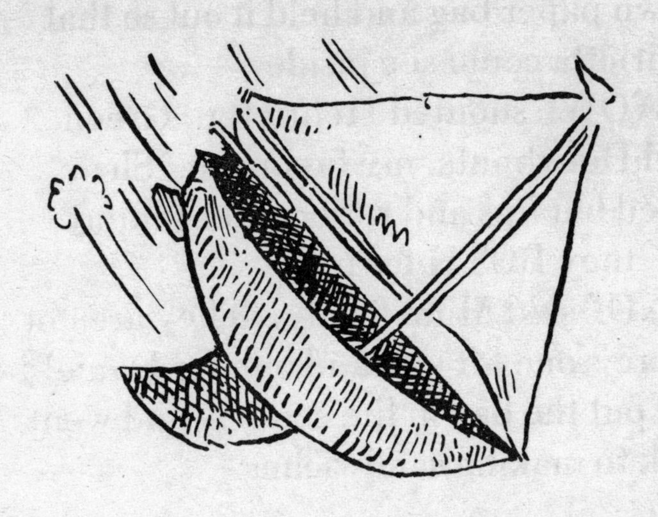

Mum looked up. 'If you're bored, Henrietta, you can always give me a hand. There's plenty to do before we go.'

'I'm not THAT bored,' muttered Henrietta.

'You could help me pack the picnic.'

Henrietta's eyes suddenly lit up. 'Picnic? You mean we're taking a picnic?'

Mum nodded. 'Yes, we are. And look what's going to be in it!' She picked up a brown paper bag and held it out so that Henrietta could see inside.

'WOW!' shouted Henrietta. 'Green Iced Doughnuts, my favourite.' She licked her lips and rubbed her tummy. 'Are they BOTH for me?'

'NO!' said Mum firmly. 'They are not. There's one for you and one for Daniel.' She put the bag in the coolbox and went back to making sandwiches.

* * *

When they got to the park, Dad took Baby-Rose for a walk round the pond, while Daniel got ready to sail his boat.

The first thing he did was to tie a piece of string onto it, so that it couldn't float away and get lost.

Then, he gently placed the boat in the water and waited for the wind to blow. He had to wait quite a long time, because it wasn't very windy.

Henrietta watched him for a while, but then got bored. She lay down on the grass and began to whistle.

'Can you stop that please, Henrietta,' said Mum. 'You sound like a kettle with toothache.'

'But I'm bored,' moaned Henrietta. 'There's nothing else to do.'

'Why don't you go and ask Daniel if you can BOTH play with his boat?'

suggested Mum.

'Because I already **KNOW** what he would say!' replied Henrietta. 'He'd tell me to get lost.'

'I'm sure he wouldn't. You go and ask him.'

Henrietta stood up and walked over to where Daniel was standing by the boating pond.

'Can we both play with the boat?' she asked, without much hope.

'Get lost!' said Daniel.

'I thought you'd say that.'

Henrietta went back and sat down on

the grass once more.

'It would be **LOVELY** if you two could play together nicely for once!' said Mum. She shook her head. 'But you don't get many miracles these days!'

* * *

She opened the coolbox and got out the Green Iced Doughnuts. She handed one to Henrietta. 'You go and give this to Daniel. Then come back here and eat yours. And we'll think of something to do.'

Henrietta checked to make sure that Daniel was getting the smallest doughnut, and then went to give it to him.

'Hey, Daniel. Here's your doughnut!'

Daniel ignored her. He was too busy watching his boat as the wind blew it along.

Henrietta waved the doughnut in front of his eyes.

'If you don't want it, I'll have it,' she said hopefully.

Daniel grunted, and without looking, put out his hand to grab the doughnut from his sister.

'OWWWWWWW!' cried Henrietta.

He had missed the doughnut. But hit her tummy!

She lost her balance and fell over onto the grass, dropping the doughnut straight into the water with a PLOP.

'My doughnut!' cried Daniel. 'It's floating away.' He tried to grab hold of it but, before he could, he tripped over Henrietta's legs and dropped the string he was holding.

'That was your fault,' he cried. 'You did it on purpose.'

At that moment Mum arrived. 'No, she didn't, Daniel. It was your fault for not watching what you were doing. You knocked her over and now you've lost your doughnut AND your boat.'

'Oh, no!' gasped Daniel. Mum was right. His boat had floated right out into the middle of the pond and was stuck against a log. 'What are we going to do?'

Henrietta stood up and smiled. 'I know what I'm going to do – I'm going to go and eat my Green Iced Doughnut.'

'Maybe you should share it with Daniel,' suggested Mum. 'That would be nice!'

Henrietta shook her head. 'He wouldn't let me play with his boat – why should I let him have some of my doughnut?'

Suddenly she wrinkled her nose.

She must have got something in it when she fell over. It was itchy.

'Aaah . . . aaah . . . Oh, no. Not my sneezy nose.' She tried to stop it but it was too late.

'ATISHOO!' She did a Henrietta hypersneeze right over the pond. That lifted the blue sailing boat high into the air, and back down again into Daniel's arms.

'You see,' giggled Henrietta, 'sailing

boats can fly!'

For a moment Daniel looked puzzled. Then suddenly he started to laugh. His soggy doughnut was wrapped around the rudder of the boat. 'So can doughnuts. Hehehe."

* * *

Five minutes later Mum walked back to the pond. 'I'm glad I brought my camera,' she said.

Daniel and Henrietta stopped playing with the boat, and looked puzzled. They were each holding half of a Green Iced Doughnut and were up to their ankles in water. 'I want to take a photograph of you two playing together *nicely*, for once!'

Henrietta turned to give her biggest smile to the camera, but suddenly slipped. Grabbing hold of Daniel to break her fall she managed to make him do a belly flop in the water.

When their mother took the photo they were *not* playing happily . . .

HENRIETTA AND THE TOOTH FAIRY
by Stan Cullimore

"Oh no. Not my sneezy nose." Henrietta tried to stop it. But it was too late . . .

Henrietta is always being naughty. She doesn't *want* to be like her sensible brother Daniel. And her sneezy nose keeps making her sneeze at all the wrong moments – at the swimming pool, buying new shoes, or trying to do good deeds. When Henrietta gets a wobbly tooth, she wants it to fall out quickly so that the tooth fairy will come. But things don't work out quite as Henrietta plans . . .

A delightful series of four stories about the mischievous Henrietta and her family – ideal for beginner readers.

'Children responded well to this lively, active book which has plenty of drawings to sustain their interest' *Federation of Children's Book Groups, Pick of the Year*

0 552 52745 9

HENRIETTA'S BUBBLE TROUBLE
by Stan Cullimore

"Yippee," Henrietta cried, as she pushed her rubber duck under the water. "I love bubbles."

Henrietta and her sensible brother, Daniel, are being given a real treat, but first she must have a bath without making any mess. That's not easy to do when you're Henrietta! Once again her sneezy nose looks as if it will land her in trouble, or will it?

A lively collection of four stories about the mischievous Henrietta and her family.

0 552 52746 7

HENRIETTA AND THE GHOST CHASE
by Stan Cullimore

"Ghosts! They're after me. HELP! They've come to chase me away."

It's a boring Sunday afternoon for Henrietta and, to make it worse, her sensible brother Daniel won't let her play his Ghost Chase game on the computer. With the help of her sneezy nose, Henrietta discovers her own version of the game – which leaves Daniel wondering if ghosts are as much fun as he thought!

A lively collection of four stories about Henrietta and her family.

0 552 52747 5